To my mother, the original dynamic granny.

By the same author

A IS FOR AAARGH!
WHO'S AFRAID OF THE GHOST TRAIN?

The Bunk-Bed Bus

Frank Rodgers

PUFFIN BOOKS

Janet's and Sam's Granny was full of energy. Every morning she put on the tracksuit that she had knitted for herself and went jogging. Janet and Sam could hardly keep up with her! Granny liked to say, "You are only as old as you feel . . . and I feel great!"

Another of Granny's favourite sayings was "You are never too old to learn."

So she learned how to work with wood and made shelves for Mum's collection of old plates. She learned how to weld metal and fixed Dad's car when it had almost fallen apart.

Mrs Grimbly-Whyte, the snooty next-door neighbour, didn't think much of Granny's efforts.
"Working with one's hands is so unladylike!" she sniffed.

But Granny didn't mind what Mrs Grimbly-Whyte said.

When Janet's and Sam's old beds fell apart (after they had been using them as trampolines), Granny told them that she'd make new ones. And she did!

She made brand-new bunk beds! Janet and Sam were delighted.
"The bunk beds will be terrific for playing on," said Sam.
"As long as you don't play trampolines," grinned Granny.

So Janet and Sam pretended that the bunk bed was a bus.
Janet drew a large sign that said . . .
THE BUNK-BED BUS. TRIPS TO THE SEASIDE. ALL
ABOARD!
Granny laughed and said, "I'll come for a trip on your bus
later, but just now I've got some work to do in the yard." And
off she bustled.

Out in the yard Granny put Janet's and Sam's old iron
bedsteads beside all the other odds and ends she had collected.
There were bits of old cars, rusty railings, an old washing-
machine, a spiral staircase, bicycle wheels, railway signals and
lots of wood.

She put her welding goggles on and started to mend Sam's bike.

Just then Mrs Grimbly-Whyte looked into the yard.

"My! What a lot of old junk you have lying around, Mrs Jones," she cooed. "Why don't you give it all to the scrap man?"

"It might come in useful one day," said Granny. "You never
know."
"That old rubbish? I doubt it!" sniffed Mrs Grimbly-Whyte.
"I spend my time doing much more ladylike things. This is my
painting of my husband Albert. I'm taking it to the Grand Art
Exhibition at the Town Hall."

"Pity you're not artistic like me, Mrs Jones," she sneered, "but, of course, you never will be because you are too old now." And with that she gave a nasty little laugh and flounced off.

Granny was furious!
"Too old?" she said. "What a cheek! What a flipping cheek!!"
Just then Janet and Sam came into the yard.
"Hello, Gran," said Janet.
"Can you come for a trip on our bunk-bed bus now?"

Granny's eyes lit up.
"Bunk-bed bus!" she exclaimed. "That's it! I'll show her!"
And, to Sam's and Janet's surprise, she rushed off into the garage.

All day long Granny worked in the garage, hammering and
clattering. Next day was the same. Then, at about two o'clock,
the noise suddenly stopped. Out came Granny.
"It's finished!" she said, and flung open the garage doors.

"I made it out of your old bedsteads and other useful bits and pieces I had lying around," she grinned.
"It's a bus!" exclaimed Sam.
"A REAL bunk-bed bus!" laughed Janet. "Gran, you are clever!"

Granny smiled proudly. "It's my sculpture for the Grand Art
Exhibition," she said. "It starts at half past two, so there's no
time to lose! Come on, give me a hand!"

So the family pushed Granny's bunk-bed bus down the High Street.

It soon became a procession as all the children from round about came running to see Granny's wonderful iron sculpture.

But when they got to the Town Hall there was a disappointment in store. The bunk-bed bus was too big to go inside.

"Sorry, madam," said the doorman, "but you'll have to leave it in the courtyard."

"Oh, no," said Granny. "Now I won't be able to take part in the art exhibition." And she sat down on the steps, looking miserable.

Janet and Sam looked at each other.
"We must do something," whispered Janet.
"Let's go inside," said Sam.
So when no one was looking they slipped through the doors.

In the main gallery the judges were examining the exhibits, paintings and sculpture of all shapes and sizes. Mr and Mrs Grimbly-Whyte stood smirking on either side of Mrs Grimbly-Whyte's portrait of her husband. They obviously

thought that it was the best thing in the whole exhibition! Then one of the judges stepped up to the microphone and cleared his throat. He was going to name the winners!

Janet could bear it no longer. She ran into the hall.
"Wait!" she shouted.
Everyone turned to see who had disturbed the proceedings.

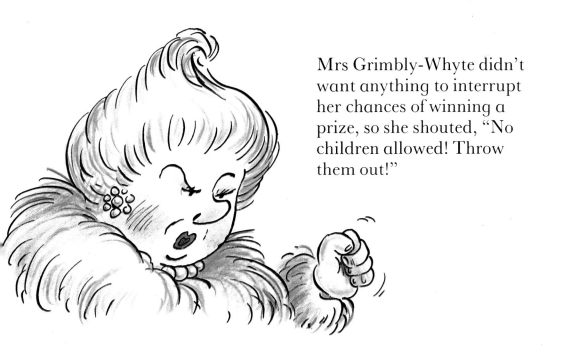

Mrs Grimbly-Whyte didn't want anything to interrupt her chances of winning a prize, so she shouted, "No children allowed! Throw them out!"

But Janet and Sam ran up to one of the judges and whispered in his ear. The judge smiled. Then he turned and spoke into the microphone. "Ladies and gentlemen," he said. "It seems that an exhibit has been overlooked. Please follow me." And he led the way outside.

Granny's bunk-bed bus was covered with children. They were having a wonderful time, and the judges agreed that this was the best piece of work in the whole exhibition.

They gave Granny first prize. She was delighted.
"How long have you been an artist, Mrs Jones?" asked the
judge.
"Since yesterday," said Granny. "I always feel you're never too
old to learn."
"How true," said the judge. "How true."

Mrs Grimbly-Whyte was
green! Her oil-painting of
her husband Albert hadn't
even been mentioned.

The Town Council bought Granny's bunk-bed bus and
installed it in the play park. Granny was very proud, and with
the money she bought something for everyone in the family.

A new jumper for Dad, a new hat for Mum, new bikes for Janet and Sam . . .

. . . and a new tracksuit and welding mask for herself! "Perhaps next time I'll build a ship," said Granny. The family didn't laugh, because they knew that with Granny nothing was impossible!